Meet **MANNY**, **SID** and **DIEGO** at their full sizes in **AMAZING LIFE SIZE** mode!

Take one of your sub-zero heroes for a walk! Make **DIEGO JUMP** or watch clumsy **SID FALL OVER**.

Take control of **SCRAT IN SPACE**! Help him find his floating acorn, and steer his **UFO**.

CARLTON KIDS

This is a Carlton Book

Ice Age: Collision Course ™ & © 2016 Twentieth Century Fox Film Corporation. All rights Reserved.

Text, design and illustration copyright © Carlton Books Ltd 2016

Published in 2016 by Carlton Books Limited. An imprint of the Carlton Publishing Group, 20 Mortimer Street, London, WIT 3JW.

A catalogue record for this book is available from the British Library.

ISBN 978 1 78312 222 6

Printed in Dongguan, China

Author: Emily Stead
Editor: Tasha Percy
Design: Darren Jordan
Design Manager: Emily Clarke
Design Director: Russell Porter
Production: Charlotte Larcombe

Picture Credits
Ice Age © 2016 Twentieth Century Fox Film Corporation

ICE AGE
COLLISION COURSE

BRING THE HERD TO LIFE

HERD THE NEWS?

Sid, Manny and their herd of sub-zero heroes are BACK! Our epic adventurers have already been brilliant babysitters, taken on dinosaurs, battled pirates and crossed continents, but now they face their biggest challenge yet.

When Scrat's acorn obsession takes him into the cosmos, he accidentally sends an enormous asteroid hurtling straight towards his home planet. The herd must figure out how to change the collision course before the asteroid hits and destroys their home forever.

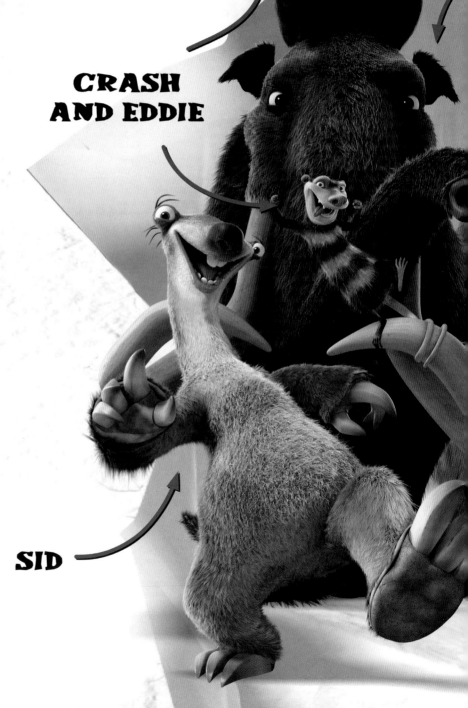

CRASH AND EDDIE

SID

Watch out! There's an asteroid heading this way.

MANNY

ELLIE

PEACHES

DIEGO

Go! Buck will
lead the way.

FRIENDS AND RELATIONS

Together, the herd tackles the toughest of challenges – but sometimes it needs a little help from new and old friends.

BUCK

When this one-eyed weasel discovers that the end of the world is nigh in *Ice Age: Collision Course*, Buck knows he must warn his friends and join the mission to save their home.

GRANNY

Sid's troublesome grandmother doesn't know the meaning of growing old gracefully – she's as much of a handful as ever!

JULIAN

A perfect match for Peaches, jolly Julian must now win over her parents. Can he prove he can protect Peaches just as well as Manny can?

SHIRA

Once a plundering pirate, Shira has left her life on the ocean waves behind her. She's happy with Diego and the herd, but is she ready for her biggest adventure yet?

7

SCRAT

Luckless Scrat is completely nuts about… nuts! It's just a shame that whenever this sabre-toothed squirrel gets his paws on one, disaster strikes. In *Ice Age: Collision Course*, Scrat's acorn antics cause a cosmic catastrophe – putting the whole planet in danger!

Scrat never speaks but the look in his eyes says it all.

HELP SCRAT IN SPACE!

Scrat is floating out in space. Can you help him find his acorn? It's there somewhere!

Somehow the acorn always slips through Scrat's frantic paws.

Chasing acorns puts Scrat in peril in *Ice Age: The Meltdown!*

SCRAT IN SPACE

Scrat has been acorn obsessed since the dawn of time, but *Ice Age: Collision Course* sees Scrat's passion take him out of this world!

One small step in space for Scrat causes a giant problem for mammal-kind back on Earth, as Scrat sends a massive meteorite heading straight towards his home planet!

SCRAT'S ACORN ESCAPADES

1 In the original *Ice Age* adventure, Scrat is frozen in a block of ice and has to chill out for a cool 20,000 years!

2 In *Ice Age: The Meltdown*, Scrat must battle an army of prehistoric piranhas to save his precious nut.

3 *Ice Age: Dawn of the Dinosaurs* sees Scrat face some pretty scary predators – dinosaurs!

4 In *Ice Age: Continental Drift*, Scrat's acorn accidentally creates a crack to the centre of the Earth, down which the scrawny squirrel slips!

MANNY

Manfred, known to his friends as Manny, is a woolly mammoth who is strong and caring, if just a bit stubborn! He may talk tough, but he'd do anything to help his friends… and often has to!

ONE OF A KIND

Before Manny met Sid, Diego and the rest of the herd, he was a bit of a loner. Having lost his family when battling with humans, he was set on going it alone, but then he bumped into a sloth called Sid who changed his mind – eventually!

INTERACTIVE MANNY

MAKE MANNY COME ALIVE!

Walk Manny around your room. You can make him life size and see how big woolly mammoths really were!

THE PERFECT MATCH

It took Manny and Ellie a little while to realize they made a perfect pair. Then along came daughter Peaches to complete their woolly family.

THE BIG HERO

Manny is a born hero – coming to the rescue is what he does best. Here are our big hero's top four massive moments.

1 Manny always does the right thing. In *Ice Age*, he saves baby Roshan and returns him safely to his family.

2 When faced with extinction in *Ice Age: The Meltdown*, Manny steps up to lead his fellow mammals to safety.

3 In *Ice Age: Dawn of the Dinosaurs*, he needs all his strength to battle some dinos who are far from being fossils.

4 When pirates attack in *Ice Age: Continental Drift*, Manny stands tall. There's no way he'll walk the plank!

PEACHES

All grown-up and ready to marry her true love, Julian, Peaches couldn't be happier. So when a giant asteroid puts their wedding plans on ice, it really feels like the end of the world for Manny's and Ellie's daughter.

> Julian and I kinda want to roam for a while.

Wasn't she cute back then?

BABY PEACHES

Peaches had a dramatic entry into the world. Her dad had to protect mum Ellie from a pack of scary dinosaurs just as Peaches was being born!

Ellie and Manny adored their baby girl!

JULIAN

Julian is madly in love with Peaches and wants to make a good impression on her parents. He's a good guy, whose hobbies include giving long power-hugs and taking things easy, but can he protect Peaches as well as Manny can?

Peaches and Julian make a perfect pair.

EMPTY NEST

Ellie and Manny have trouble believing that Julian, with his bouncy walk, is their daughter's Mr Right. They are desperate to keep Peaches close and are finding it tough admitting that Peaches can't stay their little girl forever.

WEDDING PLANNER

When news of the approaching asteroid is revealed, Peaches starts to believe that it's the universe's way of telling the mammoths they shouldn't marry. So up steps wedding-planner Sid to keep the party plans on track! How will Peaches wear her hair and what will the seating plan look like? There's so much to organize!

13

CRASH AND EDDIE

These hyperactive possums are totally extreme, and spend their time trying out dangerous stunts. They provide plenty of laughs wherever they show up.

We're smokin' hot, baby!

FUNNY FAMILY

When Crash and Eddie were just two tiny furballs, their mum adopted Ellie, a young mammoth who'd lost her family. Ellie grew up thinking she was a possum, with Crash and Eddie as her adoring brothers! Now the boys are uncles to Peaches too.

SEEING DOUBLE

This possum pair never sits still, so it's hard to tell the two apart. Here are three clues to help you work out who's who.

1 Eddie has a stripe right down the middle of his face.

2 Check out their noses – Crash's is a bit flatter than Eddie's.

3 Crash's eyes are blue, while Eddie's are brown.

STUNT TEAM

Eddie might be slightly less daring, but he always joins his crazy brother on dangerous adventures, no matter what might happen. Fear (along with common sense) is not in their DNA.

Playing dead: their tried-and-tested way to escape from predators, including scary dinosaurs.

This troublesome twosome would follow their hero Buck anywhere, even to the great beyond – if they knew what that meant.

HERD INSTINCT

It takes all sorts to make a herd. That mix of different characters and skills is the secret of the herd's success. They sometimes rub each other up the wrong way, but whenever there's a problem, teamwork saves the day.

It started with just Manny, Diego and Sid. Then came Ellie, Crash, Eddie and Peaches. New friends, such as Buck, Granny and Shira, tagged along for the ride – the herd just keeps growing!

GOING SOLO

It's not easy for a lone hunter to turn team player. Diego questioned his place in the herd when he joined up with Manny and Sid. Yet whenever his friends need him, he springs into action!

SWITCHING SIDES

Once Captain Gutt's first mate, sharp-clawed Shira jumped ship to help the herd escape in *Ice Age: Continental Drift*. Diego then persuaded the pirate she'd be happier with the herd, and Shira joined the team.

MEET THE HERD

Play with a friend! Each of you can control a different member of the herd.

INTERACTIVE TWO PLAYER

SID

With his big eyes and giant smile, Sid is a sensitive and caring sloth. Although he always tries to do the right thing, this usually lands unlucky Sid in trouble.

I'm always the first one in when there's trouble!

SUPER SID

He may not look brave at first glance, but Sid has many heroic qualities.

✴ He can create fire!

✴ He is never afraid to show his feelings and caring nature.

✴ Sid makes friends with everyone he meets – including dangerous dinosaurs.

✴ He never doubts that he'll be OK, even when he walks into the mouth of a whale!

✴ He has bags of confidence and thinks he's an example for sloths everywhere!

BRING SID TO LIFE!

Walk everyone's favourite prehistoric sloth, Sid, around the room. You can also make him life size!

HAPPY FAMILIES

Sid longs to feel like he belongs, so when his long-lost family shows up in *Ice Age: Continental Drift*, he's super happy. But his relatives soon disappear again, leaving Sid to take care of Granny!

SID'S KIDS

Sid's heart is so big that he can't help but take care of anyone in need, be it human babies, mini-sloths or dinosaur eggs. Sid even ends up playing mum to some T. rex babies in *Ice Age: Dawn of the Dinosaurs!*

19

DIEGO

This sabre-toothed hero is tricky to pin down. One minute he's a predator, the next a protector, so you never know what to expect!

INTERACTIVE DIEGO

MAKE DIEGO COME ALIVE!

Are you brave enough to release a sabre-tooth tiger? Walk him around your room and then make him life size.

TOP CAT

Diego has changed a lot since joining the herd. He's a cool cat now, but he didn't always believe in himself. Diego has got silly Sid out of so many scrapes, he feels like a super sabre!

COULD IT BE LOVE?

In *Ice Age: Continental Drift*, Diego meets the pretty pirate Shira. She left her pack, just like Diego, to make a life of her own. But Diego points out that a pack of pirates is not as good as a herd, which is more like a family.

We made it through storms and tidal waves and a vicious assortment of seafood. What more can they hit us with?

SABRE SUMMARY

Get to know Diego a little better with this lowdown on the stealthy sabre.

- He's great at tracking, picking up the scent of baby Roshan or sniffing out a momma dinosaur with ease.

- Like most cats, Diego is scared of water, but after a swimming lesson from Sid, he overcomes his fear.

- He's a mammal of many talents – from battling dinos to helping Ellie when Peaches was being born.

- When Diego met Shira his feelings were powerful – he couldn't eat or sleep – he had fallen in love.

GOING SOFT?

Diego worries that hanging out with the herd is making him lose his edge, but he comes to realize that life with the herd has actually made him stronger.

21

SHIRA

This brave big cat was once first mate in Captain Gutt's crew of brutal buccaneers. She has since left her pirate days behind her, to hang out with Diego and the herd.

Shira decided to swap the seven seas for life on dry land with Diego.

SABRE SPIRIT

- This beautiful sabre is as fast on her feet as she is a quick thinker.

- Shira was never cut out to follow orders like the other members of the crew. She'd rather be captain herself.

- After getting stranded with the herd, Shira came to realize she had met her match in Diego – in more ways than one.

- She showed her bravery, risking her life to help Diego and the herd escape the pirates.

- Shira can sometimes be seen wearing two earrings on her left ear.

GRANNY

Sid's ancient grandmother first popped up in *Ice Age: Continental Drift* and has been causing trouble ever since! She's rude, smells rotten and starts a riot whenever she opens her mouth.

> I've been struck by lightning more times than you've had hot breakfasts!

TOUGH NUT

* Sloths Granny and Sid were ditched by the rest of their family and were left to survive alone.

* Animal-lover Granny once adopted a whale and named her Precious, though none of her family believed the pet existed!

* Watch out! Granny uses her walking stick as a weapon. It's perfect for prodding and poking.

* Sid made Granny some false teeth using the jaws of a shark!

23

BUCK

Buck is back! Manny, Sid and Diego are reunited with their buddy in *Ice Age: Collision Course*, after last seeing him in the Lost World. This one-eyed weasel is built for survival, with a thirst for danger and a daredevil spirit.

> Weasled my way out of that one!

BUCK'S BEST BITS

 Buck had a close shave when he was swallowed by his arch-enemy Rudy, a beastly baryonyx in *Ice Age: Dawn of the Dinosaurs*. He made his escape by knocking out one of the dino's teeth and crawling out through his mouth.

 Buck once claimed he married a pineapple! She was ugly but he loved her.

He's nicknamed the 'Dinosaur Whisperer'.

Buck has survived breathing in toxic fumes while trying to save Sid.

THE PROPHECY

When Buck discovers a prophecy written on a stone tablet, stating that the end of the world is nigh, the herd has to take him seriously. After all, his track record of saving their bacon is 100%. Brave Buck has a plan to keep them alive – but how can one weasel overcome a 300-mile-wide asteroid?

Meet the dino-birds! Stealing dino eggs is the main interest of this trio of giant thieves. Buck must be ready at every turn to out-weasel them and protect his Lost World friends.

GAVIN is an expert flyer and poacher who always puts his family first.

His rather large daughter **GERTIE** won't hear a word said against her father.

A scrawny survivor, **ROGER** is the runt of the litter. He's both sensitive and smart.

25

JOURNEY TO GEOTOPIA

When the herd stumbles into the crystal-filled community of Geotopia in *Ice Age: Collision Course*, they meet some colourful characters. It's a peaceful paradise where time has stood still, thanks to a wall of magical crystals. The villagers there love to chill out by practising yoga and dancing to nature's song.

The Shangri-Llama has spoken.

SHANGRI-LLAMA

Like his fellow villagers, this yoga-loving llama hasn't aged a day while living at Geotopia. Manny and the herd seek answers from this wacky guy to help them on their journey, but he's too obsessed with himself to listen. Then when things go awry, the Shangri-Llama has more than a little trouble keeping his cool.

BROOKE

Beautiful Brooke can't believe it when Sid and his friends show up – she doesn't get too many visitors! A lover of flowers and rainbows, Brooke is as beautiful on the inside as she is on the outside, so it's a surprise to everyone when she finds Sid completely irresistible!

My favourite colour is rainbow!

TEDDY

Fitness-fanatic Teddy loves to keep himself in good shape, taking every opportunity to exercise. You wouldn't guess he was 326 years old! He catches the attention of Granny.

27

GLOBAL WARNING!

Manny and his friends are pretty used to global chaos. They've seen all kinds of catastrophes in the *Ice Age* movies, including avalanches, melting glaciers, volcanic eruptions and a continental drift. Now the threat level is cosmic, as a massive meteor is on a collision course to hit their home!

PLANET IN PERIL

Take one sabre-tooth squirrel, add an out-of-control nut obsession and get set for disaster. In *Ice Age: Continental Drift*, Scrat chases his acorn into the centre of the Earth, wrecking the planet and prising the herd apart.

THE BIG FREEZE

The herd's first adventure in *Ice Age* involves them trying to save a baby while the big chill of an ice age begins to freeze everything. Scrat adds to the chaos by causing an avalanche!

MELTDOWN MAYHEM

In *Ice Age: The Meltdown*, Manny and the gang race to escape from the melting ice that threatens to flood their valley. Scrat doesn't help matters by making holes in a glacier that is holding back the flood!

DINO DANGER

The herd discovers a Lost World of prehistoric predators in *Ice Age: Dawn of the Dinosaurs*. While Manny and Co. are battling dinos in the jungle, Scrat has an explosive encounter with a volcano!

OUT OF THIS WORLD!

Have you got what it takes to guide Scrat's spaceship? Help him find his beloved acorn while dodging meteors and other space objects.

5

SCRATASTROPHE!

Scrat's latest nut-hunt sees him blasted into outer space! His antics as an astronaut cause the planets to shift and send a storm of meteors heading to the herd's home. Will Scrat ever just give up and go nut-free?

LOVE IS IN THE AIR

While the temperatures may be chilly, there are plenty of heart-warming moments in the *Ice Age* adventures. Love is all around for those who look for it. And if Sid can find love, anybody can!

SABRE SWEETHEARTS

Diego and Shira have travelled a long way together since they first paired up in *Ice Age: Continental Drift*. Diego thinks he's ready to play daddy, while Shira isn't sure. She's worried that their cubs would be afraid of them due to the sabres' scary appearance.

HEAD OVER HEELS

Throughout each and every one of his *Ice Age* adventures, Sid has proved to be unlucky in love. So when a sloth as sweet-smelling and beautiful as Brooke falls for Sid at first sight, it's a bit of a shock for everyone, not least for Sid himself! Will this love story last?